REMOTE CONTROL

ADVENTURES

BOOK 1:
LOOK OUT WILD WEST!

By

Lynne M. Silber
Illustrated by Baird Hoffmire

ISBN: 1477420320
ISBN-13: 9781477420324

Library of Congress Control Number: 2012908511
CreateSpace Independent Publishing Platform,
North Charleston, SC

This book is dedicated to my wonderful husband, who has been my chief consultant, strategist and best friend through this fantastic journey and chapter in my life.

Also special thanks to Baird for the fabulous illustrations! You can check out his work at www.electricpaintbrush.com

-L.S.

Contents

Chapter 1

SPRING BREAK

"Ugh. It's raining again!" sighed Lana Landon, as she looked out the window. It was spring break, and the weather was not cooperating. After tons of phone calls, texts and emails, it seemed as though everyone Lana and her brother Zack knew were either out of town or busy doing one thing or another. Last year for spring break, the whole Landon family clan went to Florida.

What an awesome trip! Beach, sun and surf. This year, however, spring break fell later in the season. Mr. and Mrs. Landon decided to stay closer to home, since the weather in New Jersey was usually pretty mild by the end of April. *Not this year*, thought Lana, as the cold rain pounded the windowsill.

Zack trudged into the family room, looking about as sullen as Lana did.

"When is this rain going to end?" he wondered out loud. He looked over at the clock on the mantle. It was one o'clock.

Lana gave him a look.

He glared back.

"Staring out the window isn't going to make the sun come out, Lana," said Zack. "What do you want to do? Play cards?"

"No," Lana sighed again.

"How about a board game?"

"You mean *bored* game," replied Lana.

"Okay, fine. Maybe there's something on TV." Zack took the remote control from the coffee table and flopped down on the couch. He started flipping through the channels and Lana sat down next to him.

"Sports, nah. Cartoons, too babyish. How's this?"

Zack stopped on an old Western. There were cowboys and masked bandits in the middle of an old fashioned fistfight, while a stampede of buffalo rumbled in the distance. Zack paused a little too long for Lana's liking.

"This is really dumb, Zack. Give me the remote."

Lana grabbed for the remote, but Zack held it out of her reach.

"Give it to me," growled Lana.

"No, come and get it!" laughed Zack.

Lana lunged for the remote and grabbed it as Zack pulled in the opposite direction with all his might. Neither was able to hold on. The remote flew in the air like a rocket and came crashing down on the floor with a thud.

A bright green light suddenly burst forth from all sides. The kids were so shocked, they tripped over the coffee table and landed with a thud on the couch.

"Whoa, do you see that?" asked Zack, lifting his head, staring wide-eyed at the remote.

"I see it, but I don't believe it," replied a stunned Lana.

"I reckon' you never seen nothin' quite like it," said a voice.

Lana grabbed Zack's arm.

What was that?" she cried, looking around the room.

"*Who* was that, ya' mean," said the voice. "Ol' Red's my name. Look here at the TV, friends."

Zack and Lana slowly turned their heads toward the TV, and sure enough, the mystery voice was coming from the old Western they had been watching a minute before. A skinny old cowboy was staring out at Zack and Lana directly from the screen. He had grey hair and a bushy grey mustache. He wore a blue shirt, tan gloves, and a red bandana around his neck. He was squinting his eyes at the kids with a serious expression.

Lana stood and shook her head in disbelief. "This can't be possible," she said. "How can you be talking to us from the

TV?"

"That there remote is magic, my friends," said Ol' Red. "It knows when there's trouble brewin'. I reckon it can smell trouble like a bloodhound on a hot summer night."

Ol' Red leaned his face right up close to the screen. Lana and Zack took a step back.

"We need your help, kids," he said.

"Our help?" asked Zack. "With what?"

"With savin' our show, that's what," replied Ol' Red.

"What do you mean?" asked Lana skeptically.

Ol' Red began his story. "Things here in TV Land were great for a long time. There were bad guys around, but we good guys were always able to make sure every show had a happy endin'. Then, one day, things got all backwards and the bad guys started winnin' and us good guys started losin'. Just like that."

"How did that happen?" asked Zack.

Ol' Red continued. "Seems that an evil television Producer from your world got all mad at TV shows endin' good all the time. Folks are sayin' he was somehow able to find a portal into TV Land. Now he's here in our world messin' shows up, makin' sure the bad guys always win. *Unhappy* endin's is what he loves. No one knows his name so we just call him 'The Producer'. We TV folk could really use your help, kids."

Zack and Lana looked at each other.

"Um, hold that thought, Red," said Lana, pulling Zack away from the screen.

"Sure thing, take all the time you need," he replied.

Lana and Zack turned their backs to the screen and leaned their heads in toward each other.

"Okay, Zack. This is all too crazy," whispered Lana. "Talking TV characters needing our help? What will happen next? Will aliens fall from the sky?"

Zack ran his fingers through his hair in thought.

"I know it seems crazy, Lana," replied Zack. "But what if it's true? Shouldn't we at least check it out? Let's hear what Ol' Red has to say. What have we got to lose? Besides, it could be fun."

Lana looked out the window once more at the rain and made her decision. She gave Zack a nod and turned her head back toward the television screen.

"Okay Red, We're in. We'll give it a

shot," said Lana.

"Hot dog! That's what I was hopin' you'd say!" replied Ol' Red. "Okay then, pick up that there glowin' remote control, close your eyes and stand back."

Together the kids picked up the remote, closed their eyes, and held on tightly. The brilliant green glow grew larger and larger until it completely surrounded them.

Lana and Zack shielded their eyes from the blinding light, and in a flash, they were sucked into the TV.

Chapter 2

WHERE ARE WE?

When the glow of the green light subsided the kids found themselves in the middle of a desert. There were cactus plants and tumbleweeds as far as the eye could see. The dusty ground was dry and cracked. A small mountain range lay off in the distance, and a cluster of buildings lay in a valley a short walk from where the kids stood.

The sun was blazing overhead.

"Where are we?" squinted Lana, shielding her eyes from the blinding sunlight.

"My guess is we're in that old Western Ol' Red was in," replied Zack, looking around.

A few lizards scampered across the dirt by Zack's feet.

"This is so cool! We're actually in the TV!" laughed Lana. "Okay, so now that we're here? What do we do? And where is Ol' Red anyhow?"

"I don't know, Lana, but we need to find him to figure out exactly what he needs and how we can help," replied Zack. He pointed at the cluster of buildings off in the distance. "That looks like the town center. Let's start there."

"Sounds like a plan," replied Lana. "Lead on!"

The kids began walking toward the buildings when Lana stopped suddenly and looked up at the sky.

"Do you hear that?" she asked. "Sounds like thunder; weird that we'd hear thunder on such a sunny day."

The rumbling seemed to be getting louder and louder. The kids turned to look over their shoulders.

They gasped.

"That's not thunder!" cried Zack. "Remember that stampede we were watching on the TV before we were sucked in? Well, THERE IT IS! RUN FOR IT!!!"

Zack and Lana broke into a full sprint toward the town. Behind them, a large, panting, angry herd of buffalo came charging down a hill.

"Zack! We can't outrun them! Now what?" cried Lana.

"Keep running! The town is just up ahead!"

The kids ran faster and faster, but no matter how fast they ran, the stampede was closing in. At the very last second, before they were just about to be trampled into pancakes, the kids took a sharp turn to the left, a flying leap, and landed safely in a wagon filled with soft hay.

The stampede thundered past.

The kids lifted their heads and watched the herd of buffalo run through the town center.

"Whoa. That was close," panted a breathless Lana.

"Yeah, too close," replied Zack.

Lana was just about to crawl out of the wagon when, suddenly, Zack pushed Lana's head back down into the hay.

"Get down! Bandits!" he whispered.

The kids stayed out of sight as four masked bandits on horseback went riding through the town, hooting and hollering, waving lassos through the air and cracking bull whips. The kids kept their heads down until they were sure the bandits were far enough away. When all was quiet, they slowly lifted up their heads and peered over the side of the wagon.

"Bandits are never good news," groaned Lana, picking a piece of hay out from between her teeth.

"Agreed. I'm guessing those bandits are up to no good," said Zack. "And whatever they're up to,   I'm also guessing The Producer is behind it. Let's go!"

Chapter 3

UNHAPPILY EVER AFTER

The kids started walking down the main street of the town. It looked deserted; there were no people in sight. Many of the buildings were broken down. Wagons with broken wheels lay in the street. An old faded sign read '*Town of Brantley*'.

"This sure is one place I wouldn't want to go on a family vacation," said Lana, kicking aside a small pebble. "I wonder what happened to all the people?"

"We're the only ones left," said a familiar voice.

The kids turned to see Ol' Red coming out of an old building. Hanging over the doorway was a sign dangling from one rusty hinge. The sign read: Dudley's Inn. A little boy peered out from behind a woman's skirt.

"Thanks for coming," said the woman. She had long, bright red hair and a friendly smile.

"I'm Amber, and this here is my son, Dudley. I reckon you've already met my pa'. Come on inside. I'll fix y'all something to eat and we can talk about the problems we're having around here. We sure are hoping you can help us."

Amber led Zack and Lana into a modest kitchen at the far end of the inn. They sat around a small table. Amber had fixed some cold lemonade that the kids sipped thankfully. There was a small plate of hot biscuits and gravy and some beans.

"I'm sorry this is all we have," sighed Amber. "When we came to this town a few months back, there were loads of folk with children here for Dudley to play with, and lots of food. It was a real wonderful place to live. Dudley's dad, my husband Jedd, is the Sheriff in these parts. As Sheriff, it's his job to keep order in the town; and most importantly, to guard The Script."

Lana looked questioningly at Amber.

"What's The Script?" she asked.

Ol' Red put his arm around Amber and hugged her tight.

"Every show here in TV Land has its own Script the writers create," began Ol' Red. "Ours tells the story of settlers comin' out to these parts and fightin' with an outlaw group of bandits. In The Script, we townsfolk, led by Sheriff Jedd, come together like one big family and defend our homes against them bandits and drive them out once and for all."

"But that's not what happened!" said a small voice.

Zack and Lana looked over at Dudley, sitting quietly at the table.

"Them bandits kidnapped my pa', stole The Script, and all my friends left. I ain't seen my pa' in a long, long time."

A tear ran down Dudley's cheek and Amber gave him a big hug.

Ol' Red squinted his eyes at Zack and

Lana. "We need you to get The Script back for us and rewrite the endin'," he said. "It's our only hope to free Sheriff Jedd and set things right."

Zack looked confused. "So let me get this straight. This Producer guy from our world stole your Script and rewrote your show ending. But what can Lana and I do about it?"

"Yeah," seconded Lana. "I mean, we want to help, but why can't you guys find it and fix it yourselves?"

"Because," said Amber. "Only someone from *your* world can change The Script."

"The remote holds the key, kids," said Ol' Red. "Find The Script without gettin' caught by The Producer and his gang of bandits. Once you've got it, you'll rewrite the endin' so that us good guys win."

"Wait a minute," asked a skeptical Lana. "If we do this, what's going to keep The Producer from stealing The Script back when we leave?"

"Once you have changed The Script and sealed it with magic, the story can never again be changed," replied Amber.

"And I'll get my pa' and my friends back," smiled Dudley.

Lana and Zack looked at the hopeful expression on Dudley's face, and knew that they couldn't let him down. Lana bent down and tussled Dudley's hair.

"Don't worry little guy," she said. "We'll get your dad back. Pinky promise." She held her pinky up to Dudley. The little boy did the same, and they locked pinkies.

Lana and Zack looked at each other and

nodded.

"So what are we waiting for?" said a determined Zack. "Let's do it!"

Chapter 4

THE PLAN

The kids walked out of Dudley's inn looking like two real cowboys. Amber had lent them some clothes to make them look more inconspicuous. Zack was decked out in chaps and wore a leather cowboy hat on his head. Lana's fringed shirt, pants and spurred boots were a perfect fit.

Zack patted his back pocket, making sure he had the remote safely tucked away.

Ol' Red had told the kids that the bandits were holed up in a fort on the western frontier, about five miles from the town center. There were a series of tunnels under the fort. They decided that Jedd was probably being held in one of those tunnels. The kids were hopeful that once they could find Jedd, he might have some idea of where The Script was. If he didn't, well, at least they would have Jedd's help to come up with a Plan B.

That left Plan A.

Lana, Zack, and Ol' Red would ride west at sunset and camp out in the mountains just before reaching the fort. At dawn, the three would split up. Ol' Red would create some sort of diversion to get the bandits to follow him away from the fort. Zack and Lana would then sneak in, unseen, and find their way into the secret tunnels.

They would find Jedd.

They would locate The Script.

They would change the ending and put the bandits behind bars.

"But how will we actually rewrite the ending?" Lana wondered aloud as she and Zack mounted their horses. "I mean we don't have a pencil, or a pen, or anything."

"I don't know," replied Zack. He called over to Ol' Red who was just hopping up on his horse. "Red, what are we supposed to do once we have The Script. How will we know how to rewrite it? How will we know what to say? How does someone write a Script anyhow?"

Ol' Red looked at the kids with a twinkle in his eye. "Your remote holds the key," winked the old man. "As for the rest of your questions, I reckon' you'll figure it all out when the time is right. Yee haw!"

Red's horse turned on its hooves and galloped toward the mountains.

"Our remote holds the key? What key? Now what's *that* supposed to mean?" yelled Lana, but the old man was too far away to answer. Lana threw her hands up in the air and groaned.

"Do you know what he meant by that?" she asked Zack.

Zack shrugged as his horse began galloping after Ol' Red's stallion. "Beat's me!" he yelled to Lana. "Yee Haw!"

Lana spurred her horse, and the kids went galloping into the sunset.

Chapter 5

FINDING JEDD

The three friends arrived in the mountains under the cover of darkness. They quietly set up camp and tried to get some sleep before their big rescue in the morning. Ol' Red didn't have any trouble catching some shuteye, but Zack and Lana were too excited to sleep.

"What if Ol' Red's diversion doesn't work, Zack?" asked Lana. "I mean, what if we're sneaking into the fort and we come head to head with the bandits?"

Zack looked over at Red. "I think the old guy's got a trick or two up his sleeve, Lana. He'll get the job done. It's The Producer I'm worried about."

"Yeah," replied Lana. "I'm guessing this Producer guy is a smart dude if he found a way into TV Land and has been able to do what he's done. We'll have to outsmart him."

"You got it," agreed Zack.

"So if Jedd is in the tunnels, how do you think he got down there? What are we looking for?" wondered Lana.

"My guess is there's a trapdoor

34

hidden somewhere in one of the buildings," replied Zack.

Lana grinned. "I think you may be right. A trapdoor works for me! Ooooh, I'm so excited about sneaking into a real fort. It'll be like raiding the Alamo! Too bad we don't have a lasso or something in case The Producer gets wind of the fact that we're snooping around."

Zack yawned. "Yeah, I wonder what this Producer guy looks like. We may not even know if we run into him."

"Oh I doubt that," replied Lana. "My guess is he's tall, dark and scary looking."

Zack and Lana looked at each other and giggled.

"This is so weird," Lana sighed. "One minute we're bored out of our minds wishing it would stop raining, and the next minute we're in some Old Western, risking our lives to rescue the town Sheriff from some angry Producer guy who wants to make everyone in TV Land miserable."

"It's crazy," laughed Zack.

"It's unthinkable," giggled Lana.

"But here we are!" they said in unison, giving each other a high-five.

Zack settled back in his sleeping bag and tipped his hat over his eyes.

"You've got to admit; it sure has made this spring break a lot more interesting."

"Yeah," smiled Lana, closing her eyes. "You can say that again!"

Chapter 6

IS IT MORNING ALREADY?

"**Z**ack, wake up. It's time."

"The dog ate my homework. Really, Mom," mumbled Zack, still fast asleep.

Lana gave him a swift kick in the boots. "Wake up, mumblehead."

"Ouch!" grumbled Zack, rubbing his ankles. "Is it morning already?"

"Mornin' and time to ride," grinned Ol' Red.

Zack quickly jumped to his feet and dusted the earth from his pants. Lana took one last bite of a biscuit Amber had packed for her. Ol' Red looked seriously at both kids.

"You ready for this?"

"Ready as we'll ever be, Red," the kids replied, hopping up on their horses.

Ol' Red gave them one last wave and off he rode toward the fort.

"How will we know what the diversion is?" asked Lana, patting her horse's head. But before Zack could answer, the air was suddenly filled with men shouting, whips cracking, horses whinnying, and hooves pounding.

"I think that must be our diversion,"

smiled Zack. "Let's go!"

The kids galloped hard in the direction of the fort as the bandits rode the other way, following Red as planned.

The old man was wearing nothing but his underwear. He was whooping and hollering and waving his hat high above his head.

"That's awesome!" laughed Lana. "I didn't know the old man had it in him!"

Zack and Lana watched the spectacle as the posse passed them and rode out of sight.

Then all got quiet.

The kids slowed as they approached the fort. They quickly dismounted and led their horses into a wooded area, just outside the rear gate.

"This should keep them safe and out of sight," whispered Zack, stroking his horse's

nose. "Let's go."

The kids tiptoed up to the high fence and quietly slipped through an unguarded opening. The fort was relatively small and rustic. A high lookout tower rested in the center of the square. A few buildings that looked like barracks were on the far side. Nearest to the kids, a covered wagon rested under a wooded overhang, and the stables lay to their left.

"Now what?" whispered Lana.

"You take the stables," replied Zack. "I'll start with the barracks. Remember, we're looking for a trapdoor. Let's meet back here in forty-five minutes. The sooner we can find the tunnels the sooner we'll find Jedd."

"What if The Producer finds us first?" croaked Lana.

"Don't worry, if you run into any trouble, yell, ok?" replied Zack.

"Yell? *That's* your plan?" asked Lana with her hands on her hips. "Are you serious? What is *yelling* going to accomplish?"

Zack gave her a smile and a pat on the head, and then he was off.

Lana watched Zack slink around the side of the barracks and disappear through an open window. *Yell if there's trouble,* grumbled Lana, as she crept toward the stables.

Lana flattened herself against the building just outside the door and peeked in. *Coast is clear,* she thought to herself and slipped inside. She looked around. A regal looking horse was grazing inside the barn. He lifted his head to whinny as Lana crept past. She patted him on the head.

"Shh. Quiet, boy," she whispered, "Don't give me up, okay?"

The horse seemed to nod in agreement.

"You're a smart fellow, aren't you? I'll bet my allowance you're Jedd's horse. Don't worry buddy; we'll find your owner. Pinky promise."

Lana waved her pinky in the air and gave the horse a kiss on the nose. She looked around.

"Now, if I was a trapdoor, where would I be?" she asked aloud.

The horse began stomping his back hoof.

"Whoa, easy there, boy, don't get excited!"

The horse stomped again and whinnied.

"If I didn't know any better, I'd be

thinking you were trying to tell me something."

The horse whinnied again, stomped three times, and moved sideways in his stall.

"You're kidding me, right?"

Lana looked down at her feet. The floor of the stall was covered with hay and horse manure.

"Great. Couldn't you have given me the clue *before* you pooped?"

Lana rolled up her sleeves and knelt down on the floor of the stall. She turned up her nose and began moving the hay aside.

Her eyes widened in amazement. She looked at the horse. He whinnied. She looked at the floor. There was a rope handle. Lana pulled. A panel opened.

She had found the trapdoor.

"Stinky, but sweet!" she cried.

Lana peered down into the dark tunnel. There was a ladder disappearing into the darkness. She glanced at her watch. Zack would still be checking out the barracks. Lana took a deep breath, looked up at the horse, and smiled.

"Okay boy, I'm going in. Wish me luck!"

And with that, she began lowering herself into the hole.

Chapter 7

EEEK!

Zack dropped to the floor of the barracks as quietly as his boots would allow and looked around. There were a dozen cots set up in two rows of six. A few of them had disheveled blankets and looked like they had been slept in. Clothing was strewn about.

Okay, down to business.

Zack moved around the room, looking under cots, pants, boots, pillows, anyplace a trapdoor could be hidden.

Nothing.

Zack stayed low to avoid being spotted through a window. He was pretty sure Ol' Red had taken care of all the bandits, but there had been no sign of The Producer, and he sure didn't want to run into him any time soon.

He stepped over a tiny mouse scurrying across the floor. He slowly made his way to the other side of the room, feeling the walls and the floor for cracks, levers, or handles.

Still nothing.

Zack continued searching until a sound froze him in his tracks. *Someone's coming!* He looked around for somewhere to hide, and quickly dove under the nearest cot,

draping the blankets down for cover. The door of the barracks flew open as two black boots with spurs entered the room. Zack held his breath as the feet slowly walked closer to his hiding place.

"Slobs," echoed a man's voice.

The man walked over to the far side of the barracks and sat down on one of the undisturbed cots. Zack peered out between his blanket 'curtains' and silently watched a mysterious man, wearing all black, slide a dresser away from the wall. The man pulled something out from behind the dresser. From Zack's vantage point, it seemed to be a stack of papers loosely bound with twine.

The Script! Could it be?

All of a sudden, Zack felt something tickle his leg. In a panic, he looked down to find the little mouse perched on his knee.

Zack remained frozen as a mummy as the mouse sniffed his leg. The little mouse twitched it's whiskers, turned, and scurried down Zack's leg and into his boot. Sweat started beading on Zack's forehead as the mouse's soft whiskers tickled his ankle.

The man chuckled to himself, placed the papers back behind the dresser, and slid the furniture into its original place.

The mouse burrowed deeper into Zack's boot and was now tickling the bottom of his foot. Zack held his breath as tears started streaming from his eyes. *Don't laugh... don't laugh*, he begged himself.

The tickling became almost unbearable.

Just when he thought he couldn't hold in his laughter anymore, the mouse scampered out of his boot and out from under the bed.

The mysterious man whipped around at

the sound. Spotting the mouse, he mumbled something about exterminators, and walked out of the barracks, slamming the door closed behind him.

Zack exhaled and wiped the sweat from his forehead.

That was a close one!

When he was sure the coast was clear, Zack rolled out from under the bed and crept up to the dresser. Moving it aside he found a false compartment in the back, and pulled out the hidden stack of papers.

He grinned from ear to ear.

He had found The Script.

Your days are numbered, Producer, thought Zack, as he rolled up The Script and quickly shoved it under his shirt. He ran to the door, peeked his head outside to make sure the coast was still clear, and ran out of the barracks to look for Lana.

Chapter 8

THE TUNNEL

Lana's feet finally hit the ground after what seemed like an eternity. She stood still for a few minutes until her eyes adjusted to the darkness. There were a few torches burning near the ladder, which made it easier for her to see that the tunnel went in two directions.

Lana took one of the lit torches out of its holder and stood for a minute, considering which tunnel to follow. *I really should get*

Zack, she thought to herself; but curiosity got the best of her and she couldn't resist. *Taking a quick look around can't hurt, right?*

She looked in both directions. Neither passage looked particularly inviting. *Eenie meenie, miney moe.* She waved her finger back and forth, pointing left, then right, then left again.

Oh, good grief, I'll just go right.

Lana turned and began following the tunnel through the darkness. She ran her hands over the smooth stones that lined the walls. The tunnel was well made, not just dug into the dirt, but also fortified with stone and wooden beams. *Whoever made this tunnel really knew what they were doing,* she thought to herself.

She followed the tunnel's twists and

turns and saw the faint glow of a light ahead of her. Not wanting to be seen, Lana quickly stomped out the torch and hid in the shadows. The light seemed to be coming from a room up ahead. Lana slithered along the wall until she was just outside what appeared to be a jail cell of some sort. She peeked around the corner.

Without warning, a hand reached out from between the bars and grabbed Lana by the arm.

Lana let out a yelp as the owner's other strong hand clamped over her mouth.

She wiggled and squirmed, but it was no use. She was pinned against the bars.

"Shhh. I'm not gonna hurt you," said a voice. "If you promise not to yell, I'll

uncover your mouth."

Lana nodded and the hand slowly pulled away. The stranger was a scruffy but nice looking man in a cowboy hat. Lana could imagine only one person who would be locked down in the catacombs like this.

"Jedd?" she whispered to the stranger.

The man drew his other hand back behind the bars and looked at Lana suspiciously.

"How do you know my name?" he asked.

"I'm here with my brother, Zack," said Lana. "Ol' Red and Amber sent us."

Jedd smiled at the thought of his family and nodded gratefully to Lana.

"I've been down here for some time. I sure am glad to see you. How did you know where to look for me?" questioned Jedd.

"Oh, a little birdie told me," replied Lana. "Actually, it was a horse, but that's beside the point. We need to get you out and *fast* before the evil creepy Producer guy finds out I'm down here."

"*It's a little late for that, young lady,*" said a deep, menacing voice.

Lana cringed as two strong hands wearing black gloves grabbed her arms from behind.

"The Evil Creepy Producer Guy, at your service," said the voice.

Lana started to turn, but before she could take a good look at The Producer, she felt a boot to her back and she tumbled face first into Jedd's cell.

The sound of bars slamming and keys jingling rang in her ears.

"I had heard there were some pesky kids

from my world nosing around," said The Producer, whose face still remained in the shadows.

"I have no idea how you got here, but it doesn't seem to matter now, does it? Whomever you are, you are in *there*," he said, pointing at the cell. "And I am out *here*." He laughed a very sinister laugh. "You lose, I win, and that is certainly a perfect *unhappy* ending, now, isn't it?"

The laughing continued echoing in Lana's ears even after The Producer had walked away and disappeared down the tunnel.

"You okay?" asked Jedd, picking Lana up and helping her dust off.

"Yeah, the only thing wounded is my pride," said Lana, looking around at the dark, musty jail cell. "This is definitely NOT how I imagined I'd be spending my spring break."

Jedd looked at Lana with a puzzled expression.

"Never mind," groaned Lana.

Chapter 9

THE RESCUE

Zack looked at his watch. *Where in the world is Lana,* he wondered, pacing back and forth. With The Script in hand, all they needed to do was figure out how to rewrite the ending and everything would be back the way it was supposed to be. But he had no idea how to do that himself, and he needed Lana's help to try and figure it out. They hadn't found Jedd yet either, and they had made a promise to Dudley that they would bring back his dad. That was one promise Zack intended to keep.

I'd better check and make sure Lana's okay, Zack thought to himself. He ran across the courtyard and flattened himself against the stables, just outside the door. He peeked his head inside to be sure The Producer wasn't anywhere in sight. The coast was clear, so he slipped silently inside. The trapdoor that Lana had found was still open, and a fine looking horse was inside the barn whinnying.

Well, I'll be, thought Zack. *She found the trapdoor! Well done, Lana!*

Zack took a moment to pat the whinnying horse on the nose, and slowly lowered himself down the ladder into the catacombs. He made his way through the tunnels, feeling the walls as he walked deeper and deeper into the maze. The air grew moist and cool and a chill ran through Zack's body, making him shiver with dread. *What if something really bad had happened to Lana?* He shook his head, trying to clear the unpleasant thought.

He continued in the darkness until he spotted a faint glow at the end of the tunnel. Ever so silently, he crept closer and closer to the light.

"HELP! Police! SWAT! Haz-Mat, ANYONE!" screamed a voice.

Zack gave a sigh of relief and ran to the end of the tunnel.

"See!" laughed Zack. "I told you if you got into trouble all you had to do was yell!"

"Very funny," glared an annoyed Lana.

"Jedd, meet Zack. Zack, meet Jedd. Now do something to get us out of here!"

Zack looked around the cell and pulled at the bars.

"Don't you think we've already tried that?" snorted Lana, rolling her eyes at her brother.

"Okay, okay, give me a minute to think."

Zack looked around for keys, or something to pick the lock with. Nothing.

"Is there anything useful in the cell with you?" asked Zack.

"Nope," replied Jedd. "I've been trying for weeks to get out of this box."

"Wait a minute," said Zack, his eyes lighting with realization. He pulled The Script out from under his shirt.

"Is that what I think it is?" asked a wide-eyed Lana.

"The Script! Well I'll be!" exclaimed Jedd. "Where did you find it? I tore this fort apart looking for it before I was caught by them bandits."

"It was in the barracks, in a secret compartment," replied Zack.

"I can't believe you found it!" said Lana. "But how is it going to get us out of here before The Producer comes back?"

An excited Zack dropped to his knees and started frantically turning the pages.

"Right here on page seventy-six!" Zack continued. "Here is where Jedd gets thrown into the dungeon and locked up! If we can rewrite this part, we can get you guys out of there and figure out how to change the rest of the story!"

Lana dropped to the dirt to examine The

Script with Zack.

"Okay, so it says, '*The door slammed behind Jedd with a thunderous crash as the lock turned, sealing his fate.*' Well, that's not very nice," said a sarcastic Lana. "So now what do we do? Uh, you got something to write with, brother genius?"

Zack pulled the remote from his back pocket.

"Lana, I don't think we actually need something to write with! Remember what Ol' Red said? He said the remote holds the key! Its magic will help us rewrite the story! I have an idea."

Zack pointed the remote at The Script.

"Um, so let's say something like, '*Just as it seemed as if there was no hope for Jedd, there was a squeaking noise and a mouse carrying a key scampered across the floor.*'"

Lana glared at Zack.

"Give me a break, Zack! That's the dumbest thing I've ever—"

But before she could finish her thought, the remote started to glow and new words began appearing on the page.

"I don't believe this!!!" exclaimed an excited Lana. "It's working! Far out!"

Just as quickly as the words magically changed on the page, a squeaking noise came from the other end of the tunnel. A little mouse scampered toward them, carrying something shiny between its jaws.

"That's amazing!" said Jedd, staring out from between the bars at the little rodent. "Keep it going, friends!"

Zack continued. "Okay, how about, '*The mouse ran through the bars into the dark, musty cell and dropped the key at Jedd's feet.*'"

The mouse ran into the cell and dropped the key.

"This is so cool!" said an excited Lana. "Let me try. Okay, I'll say something like, '*Jedd smiled at the mouse, patting its little head just before it scampered away back into the darkness. Jedd lifted the gleaming key and slipped it into the lock. He heard a loud click and the bars swung open. Saved at last!*' Tah Dah!"

As if entranced, Jedd patted the little mouse's head, picked up the key, placed it in the lock, and turned.

The door swung open.

"We did it!" exclaimed Zack. "Now

let's change the ending and set things back the way they were!"

Voices overhead cut through the kids' concentration. Jedd, Lana and Zack looked up at the ceiling of the tunnel.

"Uh oh," groaned Lana. "I think The Producer and his rowdy band of outlaws are on to us."

"Let's get out of here!" cried Zack. "We've got to get somewhere safe to read the rest of The Script!"

"Right behind you, Zack," replied Jedd. "Let's move!"

The three raced back through the dark tunnel toward the ladder.

Chapter 10

HOT PURSUIT!

Lana poked her head out from the trapdoor and looked around the stables. "Coast is clear," she whispered, as she climbed the rest of the way out of the hole. Zack and Jedd followed close behind. Jedd stood, squinting at the bright sunshine streaming in through the windows.

"It's been a long time since I've seen any sunshine," smiled Jedd, soaking in the sun's rays.

He walked over to his horse.

"Hey there, Lightning, my friend," he said, scratching the horse behind its ears. Lightning nuzzled Jedd and gave a snort.

"Okay, I'm all for happy reunions, but we really need to get out of here before we're found out!" said Lana, nervously.

Zack quickly turned to Jedd. "Jedd, ride Lightning out of here. We'll meet you back in town."

"Will do!" Jedd tipped his hat at the kids and leapt atop Lightning.

"See y'all real soon, and be careful!"

Jedd gave Lightning a loud "*Yee Haw*" and galloped at full speed toward the main gate. Hollers and shouts came from various buildings in the fort as the bandits began running toward the escaping Jedd.

"Don't let him get away, you fools!" shouted an all too familiar voice.

"It's The Producer," cried Lana. "Let's get out of here!"

Lana and Zack sprinted out the back door of the stables toward the opening at the rear of the fort. Since all of the attention was directed toward Jedd, it wasn't hard for the kids to sneak back out into the woods unseen.

Thankfully the horses were still where the kids had left them. They quickly climbed up into the saddles. Zack patted down his pants and shirt, making sure the remote and The Script were safe and wouldn't fall out somewhere along the way.

"Let's go!" he shouted.

The horses seemed to know exactly where they were headed and ran like two steam trains roaring down a track. Hooves thundered and the kids held on for dear life.

A giant shadow flew out of nowhere as Jedd's mount came leaping down from a mountainous trail and joined the kids' mad dash toward town. Then Ol' Red and his mount came galloping over from a nearby pass to join the group.

The four riders and their horses galloped at full speed, kicking up a blinding dust cloud behind them.

Zack and Lana looked back and saw the bandits emerge from the dust.

"Faster!" cried Lana. "They're gaining on us!"

Sensing the urgency, the horses picked up their pace.

"The town's right up ahead!" shouted Jedd over the pounding of hooves. "We'll split off! Find a safe place in town to hide so you can do your magic, kids, and Red and I will distract them bandits. They're really beginning to get on my nerves."

Jedd and Ol' Red careened off to the left, directing the bandits away from Zack and Lana as their horses continued to gallop toward the town.

Lana sighed with relief and glanced over her shoulder, expecting to see no one pursuing them. To her dismay one single rider still followed. He was dressed in black from head to toe, riding a slick, black stallion, and would have fit in perfectly with the surroundings if not for the black mirrored sunglasses that gave him away immediately.

"It's The Producer!" shouted Lana. "He's coming to get us!"

Zack and Lana rode like the wind until they were in the center of town. They quickly slowed their mounts, hopped off, and sprinted into the first building they came to, barely noticing the sign overhead which read: Nifty's Saloon.

They leapt over the bar and crouched down low, hoping they could work their magic before The Producer found them.

Ripping The Script out from under his shirt, Zack flipped furiously through the pages until he came to the last scene.

"Here it is," he whispered to Lana.

"Do it quick!" Lana cried suddenly, as she heard the swinging doors of the saloon crash open.

"End of the line, you meddlesome kids,"

roared The Producer. "I know you're in here."

With a quick flick of his wrist, The Producer cracked his bull whip in the air, aiming it at the mirror behind the bar. The mirror shattered into a thousand tiny fragments. The kids ducked under the sink behind the bar for safety as the glass fell to the ground.

"*So* sorry it has to end like this," bellowed The Producer.

"Not as sorry as *you* will be, Producer," yelled a female voice.

The kids peered over the bar.

Amber was standing behind The Producer, twirling a lasso high above her head. Before The Producer knew what hit him. Amber flung the lasso high in the air. It landed perfectly over The Producer's

body. Amber pulled the rope tight, trapping The Producer's arms under the lasso. The bull whip fell to the ground with a thud.

"Now, kids!" shouted Amber.

Zack and Lana quickly stood up. Zack grabbed the remote from his back pocket and pointed it at The Script.

Brother and sister began chanting in unison, "*Sheriff Jedd and Ol' Red rounded up all the bandits and put them in jail where they belonged.*"

"NOOOO!" cried The Producer, struggling to free himself from the lasso.

As the remote glowed, the kids continued. "*Never again did the bandits bother the peaceful town of Brantley. The townsfolk returned and everyone lived happily ever after. The End.*"

Upon uttering the final words, a blinding

burst of green light exploded in the saloon. Zack and Lana shielded their eyes from the glare as a fading voice cried,

"I'll get you for this! You haven't seen the last of me!"

In a flash, The Producer disappeared.

Chapter 11

HAPPILY EVER AFTER

When Zack and Lana opened their eyes, the sight amazed them. The saloon was bursting with excitement and life. Men were playing cards, rolling dice, and patting each other on the back. Lana and Zack looked at each other in wonder.

"The people! They came back!" cried

Lana excitedly.

They walked outside to a scene equally as fantastic. Wagons rolled by and children laughed in the streets, while women were briskly walking along chatting to one another.

Zack opened The Script, and sure enough, the last page had been changed and the words **'THE END'** glowed in bright, green letters.

Looking past the wagons, the kids spotted Amber, Ol' Red, and Sheriff Jedd walking toward them. A happy Dudley rode atop his daddy's shoulders.

Zack smiled at Jedd and handed him The Script.

"I think this belongs to you," he said.

Jedd nodded and happily took The Script from Zack.

"I reckon' we owe you kids a great deal of thanks," said Jedd. "Y'all saved our town, and really did give us a happy ending."

"How can we ever repay you?" asked Amber, as she hugged Lana.

"You gave us an adventure we'll never forget," replied Lana. "I'm glad we could help."

"What about The Producer?" wondered Zack. "I mean, he just kind of disappeared. What do you think happened to him?"

"Oh, I'm sure he'll turn up on another show sooner or later and mess things up again," replied Ol' Red, shaking his head.

Zack put a reassuring hand on Red's shoulder.

"When he does, we'll be ready; *that's* for sure," he replied.

Zack took the remote out of his back pocket. It was glowing with the same iridescent green light that had brought them into TV Land.

"I think it's time for us to go home," said Zack.

Lana reached up and tussled Dudley's hair. "You be a good boy, you hear?" she said.

Dudley nodded and hugged his dad's head. Amber, Jedd, Dudley and Ol' Red waved goodbye, turned and walked into Dudley's Inn.

Lana and Zack sighed and looked around the bustling town of Brantley for the last time. They smiled at each other, and held on tightly to the remote as the green glow grew larger and larger until it completely surrounded them.

In a blinding flash of light they disappeared.

Chapter 12

BACK HOME

When the kids opened their eyes, they were standing in the middle of their family room wearing their own clothes.

They looked up at the TV just in time to catch a big **'THE END'** over the last scene of the Western.

Zack turned off the television and put

down the remote. The kids looked at each other, too stunned to even speak. They stood there for a long time.

"Zack, that was such an amazing adventure!" whispered Lana.

Zack looked over at the clock on the mantel. It still said one o'clock.

"Lana, no time passed! It's as if nothing ever happened! That's so weird," said Zack, running his fingers through his hair in thought.

Lana smiled at her brother. "But something *did* happen. Something pretty incredible."

Lana's smile changed to a frown, and she looked seriously at her brother. "Zack, do you think The Producer will really show up somewhere else in TV Land, and someone else might ask for our help, like

Ol' Red predicted?"

"I bet he will, Lana," replied Zack, nodding. "But now that we know how the remote's magic works, and how rewriting The Script can totally change a story, we'll know what to do the next time for sure."

"I hope he messes up something at the beach next time. Something that has to do with surf boards and getting a suntan," teased Lana.

Zack shook his head and rolled his eyes at his sister.

The phone rang.

"Hey, Zack, Lana," called their Mom from down the hall. "Alex and Emma are on the phone and they want to know if you want to go over to their house and hang out."

Lana and Zack smiled at each other.

"Sure, Mom; tell them we'll be right over!" called Zack.

The kids gave each other a big high five, grabbed their jackets, and dashed out of the house.

THE END.

To learn more about Zack, Lana and their upcoming adventures visit them at:

WWW.REMOTECONTROLADVENTURES.COM

Hi! My name is Lynne Silber and I'd like to tell you a little about myself! I worked in the fast paced environment of live entertainment television for ten years. Basically, I made TV shows! It was a fun and exciting career. I met many interesting people along the way, many of whom are the inspiration for the characters in my books. I have always loved TV. When I was a child I often wished that I could zoom into my television and become part of the show...I mean, how cool would that be? Well, I have taken my childhood dream and brought it to you through Zack and Lana's Remote Control Adventures. I hope you enjoy reading them as much as I enjoy writing them! When I am not writing, I like to spend time tending to my vegetable garden and running after my three wonderful children and our two spunky kittens, Misty and Fluff!

18117551R00060

Made in the USA
Middletown, DE
22 February 2015